Dirty Bertie

RATS!

For Tim and Sarah ~ D R

For Mark and Sarah – wishing you a long and

happy married life together! ~ A M

STRIPES PUBLISHING
An imprint of Little Tiger Press
1 The Coda Centre, 189 Munster Road,
London SW6 6AW

A paperback original
First published in Great Britain in 2014

Characters created by David Roberts
Text copyright © Alan MacDonald, 2014
Illustrations copyright © David Roberts, 2014

ISBN: 978-1-84715-441-5

Printed and bound in the UK.

10 9 8 7 6 5 4 3 2 1

Dirty Bertie
RATS!

DAVID ROBERTS WRITTEN BY ALAN MACDONALD

stripes

Pants!
Burp!
Yuck!
Crackers!
Bogeys!
Mud!
Germs!
Loo!
Fetch!
Fangs!
Kiss!
Ouch!
Snow!
Pong!
Pirate!
Scream!
Toothy!
Dinosaur!
Zombie!
Smash!
My Joke Book
My Book of Stuff

Contents

CHAPTER 1

"Did you know rats eat their own poo?" asked Bertie, over breakfast.

Suzy pulled a face. "MUM! Bertie's being disgusting!" she moaned.

"I'm not," said Bertie. "I saw it on TV. Rats are amazing. You can flush them down the toilet and they still survive!"

"We don't want to know, Bertie,"

sighed Mum.

Bertie poured Puffo Pops into his bowl. He didn't see why no one liked rats. Actually they were a whole lot cleaner than humans. You didn't see humans picking fleas off each other.

"You're dropping cereal everywhere," said Suzy.

Bertie looked down to see a trail of Puffo Pops on the table.

"It's not my fault," he said. "There's a hole in this box."

Mum took it from him. It looked like the corner of the box had been nibbled away.

"Did you do this, Bertie?" asked Mum.

"No – why do I always get the blame?" asked Bertie.

Mum frowned. Getting down on her knees she poked her head into the cupboard.

"Oh no!" she groaned. "MICE!"

"Where?" cried Bertie.

"There," said Mum. "Those are mouse droppings!"

"EWWW!" cried Suzy, putting down her spoon.

Bertie went over to look. He had never seen mouse droppings before. They were small brown pellets, a bit like hamster or rat droppings.

"Don't touch them!" warned Mum. "They're covered in germs – you'll catch something!"

Dad came in as they were taking all the tins out of the cupboard. "What's going on?" he asked.

"We've got mice," said Mum.

"You're joking!"

"No," said Bertie. "They've left tiny poos in the cupboard. Have a look!"

"No thanks," said Dad. "Are you sure it's mice?"

"It could be rats," said Bertie, hopefully.

"It's definitely mice,' said Mum,

standing up. "The question is, what do we do about it?"

"I like mice," said Bertie. "Can I keep one?"

"NO!" shouted Mum and Dad at once.

"Why not?"

"Because mice are pests," said Mum. "They nest in the walls."

"Once they move in they start having babies," warned Dad.

"REALLY?" said Bertie.

This sounded brilliant. He would have liked a rat but a mouse was the next best thing – and baby mice would be even better! He could train them to play mouse football or to juggle lumps of cheese.

"Right," said Dad. "I'll get some poison."

"POISON!" howled Bertie.

"That's cruel!" said Suzy.

"And dangerous too," said Mum. "What if Whiffer eats it?"

Dad hadn't thought of that. Whiffer ate anything he found on the floor.

"Okay. Then I'll buy a mousetrap," said Dad.

"What for?" moaned Bertie. "I said I'll look after them!"

"How many times do I have to tell you – mice are not pets!" said Mum.

"They are, Trevor's got one," Bertie argued.

"I don't care," said Mum. "We are NOT having mice in the house."

"They're disgusting," said Dad. "They eat all the food and leave their mess everywhere."

Dirty Bertie

Bertie didn't see why everyone was making such a big fuss. Mice had to poo somewhere. Besides, if he had a pet mouse he'd make sure it was house-trained. He would make it a teeny-weeny toilet the size of a matchbox.

"Please!" he begged. "Just one little mouse."

"NO!" said Mum firmly. "No mice and that's the end of the matter."

CHAPTER 2

When Dad got home from work he had something to show them.

"There we are, one mousetrap," he said, putting it on the table.

Bertie stared. He'd never seen a mousetrap before. It was a flat wooden block with a metal handle on a spring. It came with instructions.

"What does it mean, 'snap'?" Bertie wanted to know.

"That's how it works," said Dad. "I'll show you." He pulled the metal handle back until it clicked. "The mouse comes sniffing around and smells the bait," he explained. "Sooner or later he hops up here to take a nibble and…"

SNAP! The metal handle flew back as he poked it with a pencil.

Bertie stared. "But that's horrible! You'll kill it!" he argued.

"I certainly hope so," said Mum.

"That's the point. It's a mousetrap," said Dad.

"But can't you just catch it, then let it go outside?" Bertie pleaded.

Mum shook her head. "We don't want it coming back, we want to get rid of it once and for all."

Bertie scowled at the mousetrap. "Well, I think it's murder," he said. "And don't blame me if a ghost mouse comes back to haunt you."

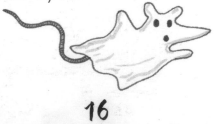

Dirty Bertie

Upstairs Bertie lay on his bed, thinking.
It wasn't fair — what had the mouse ever
done to them? If it was up to him he'd
think of a way to catch the mouse alive.
Bertie sat up suddenly. Yes, why not?
He could make his own mousetrap.
He went to his wardrobe and pulled out
an old shoebox from under his clothes.

Dirty Bertie

Twenty minutes later he put down
the scissors and admired his work.

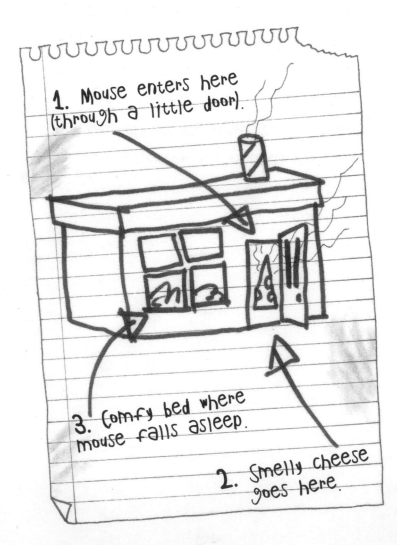

Dirty Bertie

Bertie had it all planned. He'd wait till everyone was asleep and then sneak down to the kitchen. Dad's nasty old mousetrap could go in the bin and the Super-Safe Mouse Catcher would take its place.

Bertie would have to get up early tomorrow morning to find out if his plan had worked. It was probably better not to mention anything to Mum and Dad. The mouse could live under his bed – at least until he had house-trained it, anyway.

CHAPTER 3

Bertie woke up. Light was spilling through his bedroom curtains. What time was it? Oh no! He shot out of bed – he had to get down to the kitchen before anyone else.

Downstairs the Super-Safe Mouse Catcher was still where he'd left it. Bertie tiptoed closer and kneeled down. Holding his breath, he listened for mousey squeaks. Nothing. He lay on his belly and peeped through the tiny doorway. The lump of cheese had vanished. But there, asleep in a heap of tissue paper, was something small, brown and furry.

Dirty Bertie

Bertie could hardly believe it. His mouse catcher had actually worked! Wait till he told Darren and Eugene about this! Carefully he lifted the shoebox and scooped up the sleepy little mouse. It twitched in his hand. Just then he heard footsteps on the stairs. Someone was coming! Quickly he replaced the mouse, jammed on the lid and hid the box behind his back.

"Oh Bertie! You're up early," said Mum.

"Yes, I was just um ... getting a drink," said Bertie. "I'm going back to bed now."

Mum frowned. "What's that?" she said.

"What?"

"That thing you're hiding behind your back."

"Oh this," said Bertie, bringing out the shoebox. "It's, you know ... just a box."

Dirty Bertie

Mum folded her arms. "What's in it?"

"Nothing!" said Bertie.

The lid moved. The mouse must have woken up. Mum was staring at the box.

"Open it," she said.

Bertie sighed. It was no use arguing, he'd been rumbled. He removed the lid.

Mum peeped inside. "EEEEK!"

Dirty Bertie

"SHH! You'll scare him!" said Bertie. "He's only just woken up."

"It's a mouse!" said Mum. "Where did you get him?"

Bertie proudly explained how he'd made the Super-Safe Mouse Catcher where he'd found Monty asleep.

"Monty?" said Mum.

"That's his name," said Bertie. "Isn't he cute? Look at his little paws!"

Mum shook her head. "I know what you're after, Bertie, but you are not keeping him."

"He's tiny! He won't be any trouble!" pleaded Bertie.

"NO!" said Mum. "He's got to go."

Bertie looked sadly at Monty, who was now sniffing around his box.

Dirty Bertie

"I won't let him out," he promised. "He can stay in my bedroom!"

"Not a chance," said Mum. "Take him outside and let him go. And don't do it anywhere near the house!"

Bertie took the box to the back door. It wasn't fair. He never got to keep any of his pets. Even when he tried to keep dog fleas his mum squashed them. He went outside. Mum had said to release Monty away from the house, but where exactly? If the mouse got next door, the Nicelys' mean old cat might catch him.

Bertie looked round the garden. Where would be safest? The flower beds? The vegetable patch? No, of

course, the shed! It wasn't near the
house and better still it was filled with
piles of junk. Nobody would notice a
tiny little mouse house hidden under a
blanket. If he was careful he could visit
Monty every day!

CHAPTER 4

Next morning, after breakfast, Bertie
sneaked out to the shed. He'd saved
Monty some peanut butter on toast.

"Monty! Monty?" he called.

He lifted up an old blanket to uncover
the shoebox.

"You stay here, Monty," he explained,
feeding him bits of toast. "I've got to go

to school, but I'll see you later."

He watched the mouse nibble his breakfast. It seemed a pity to leave him all alone. Then Bertie had an interesting thought. He looked down at his school bag. The shoebox would just about fit inside. He could cover it with his PE kit and Miss Boot would never suspect a thing.

On the way to school Bertie met up with Darren and Eugene.

"You'll never guess what I've got in my bag," he said, grinning.

"What?" said Eugene.

Bertie took off his backpack and pulled out the shoebox. Carefully he lifted the lid.

Darren and Eugene peered inside.

Monty blinked up at them.

"A mouse!" gasped Darren. "Where'd you get him?"

"I caught him," said Bertie, proudly. "We found mouse droppings in our kitchen so I made my own mouse catcher. He's called Monty."

"Cool," said Eugene. "What are you going to do with him?"

"Keep him," said Bertie. "He's coming to school."

Eugene stared. "Miss Boot will go bonkers. Have you forgotten she's terrified of rats?"

"So what? He's a mouse," said Bertie.

"Same thing," said Darren. "She'll go nuts if she sees him."

"She won't," said Bertie, closing the lid. "He can stay in here and we'll take him out at break to play with him."

Later that morning Miss Boot was droning on about living in Tudor times. Bertie thought she was probably old enough to remember them. He hadn't checked on Monty for at least ten minutes. Reaching into his bag, he brought out the shoebox and took off the lid.

YIKES! Where was Monty?

Bertie emptied the contents of his bag on to the floor. Lunch box, pencils, socks, mouse droppings … but no mouse.

"What's up?" hissed Darren.

"He's escaped!" said Bertie.

"Who has?"

"Monty, you dumbo! He's not in his box."

They passed the message to Eugene and the three of them searched under their desks. No luck. Darren nudged Bertie and pointed to the front.

"What?" hissed Bertie.

"There! On Miss Boot's desk," said Darren.

Bertie stared in horror. A neat trail of mouse droppings led across Miss Boot's desk to Monty, who sat there nibbling the register. Bertie had to do something before it was too late. He jumped to his feet.

"MISS!"

Miss Boot glared at him. "What is it now, Bertie?"

"I've lost my ... er ... my pen!" said Bertie.

"Well, borrow one from someone else," sighed Miss Boot.

"But it's my best pen, I need to look for it," begged Bertie.

"SIT DOWN!" thundered Miss Boot.

Bertie sat down. Monty had vanished from the teacher's desk. Where had he got to now? Bertie caught sight of something streaking across the floor.

"Now," said Miss Boot. "I want you to write down this— AARGHHH!"

She gave a yelp. Something was tickling her ankle. The ticklish feeling crept up the back of her leg. She tried to ignore it…

"I want you to write this— OOOH … HEE-HAA!" she squawked.

The class stood up to get a better view. Their teacher was dancing around as if her pants were on fire. Something brown and furry shot up her skirt.

"AARGGHHH! A RAT!" she screamed.

Bertie wouldn't have believed that Miss Boot could move so fast. One moment she was hopping around like a jumping bean – the next she had leapt on to her desk.

"A RAT! A RAT!" she shrieked. "DO SOMETHING!" This was Bertie's chance. He grabbed the shoebox and leaped into action. A mad chase broke out as Bertie scrambled under chairs and tables and Monty tried to escape.

At last he managed to get Monty back in the box.

"It's okay, Miss, I've got him," Bertie

panted. "He can't get away."

Slowly Miss Boot climbed down off her desk and smoothed out her skirt. She shuddered.

"I hate rats!" she said.

"But he's not a rat, he's a mouse," said Bertie. "His name's Monty."

Miss Boot turned her head. She gave Bertie a long hard look. "And how exactly do you know his name?" she demanded.

Bertie gulped. *Ooops! Now he really was in trouble.*

CHAPTER 1

Bertie sat down and pulled off his trainers with a groan. He thought PE was meant to be fun. Somebody should tell Miss Boot that. She'd just put them through an hour of star jumps, squats and sit-ups.

"It is obvious that many of you are not fit," she said. "Too many crisps and

too much TV. What you need is fresh
air – that's why this Friday we are going
to be doing cross-country."

Bertie rolled his eyes. What new form
of torture was this?

"Who can tell me what cross-country
is?" asked Miss Boot.

Know-All Nick was bouncing up and
down as if he might burst. "Miss, Miss

I know!" he panted. "Is it like a race?"

"Very good, Nicholas," said Miss Boot. "Cross-country is a race run over fields and paths. Who'd like to try it?"

Class 3 looked at the floor.

"I see," said Miss Boot. "And who'd rather stay inside and practise one hundred spellings?"

No one spoke.

"Good, then remember to bring your PE kit on Friday. What do you need on Friday, Bertie?"

"Um … sandwiches?" said Bertie.

"PE KIT!" thundered Miss Boot. "Do NOT forget! Next month it's the County Cross-Country Trials and we will be taking part. I want four good runners for the team."

Bertie didn't know where Miss Boot was going to find them. Most of the class were slower than a tortoise with a limp. Trevor Trembleton usually brought a note when it came to PE and Know-All Nick was weedier than a stick insect. Nick was the only boy Bertie knew who could play football without getting mud on his kit.

CHAPTER 2

At break time Bertie and his friends
leaned against the railings.

"Cross-country," sighed Eugene. "Isn't
that really tough?"

"Don't ask me," said Bertie. "Why
can't we do something fun like beach
volleyball?"

Bertie had seen beach volleyball on TV.

It looked brilliant, but the school didn't have a beach – or a volleyball, for  that matter.

"Anyway," said Darren. "At least we won't be in the cross-country team. Miss Boot will pick the fastest runners."

"I don't know, I'm pretty speedy," said Bertie.

"Pretty *weedy*, you mean," said a voice.

Bertie looked round to see his old enemy, Know-All Nick. Didn't he have anything better to do than listen in on other people's conversations?

"Mind your own business," said Bertie.

Nick took no notice. "Since when were you a fast runner?" he sneered.

Bertie stuck out his chin. "I'm faster than you."

"Really? Who was first back to the coach after swimming last time?" said Nick. "Oh yes, it was me!"

"Only because you cheated," said Bertie. "I'd like to see you do cross-country. You couldn't cross the road."

"Actually, I'm probably the fittest in the class," boasted Nick. "Because I eat all my vegetables!"

"You look like a vegetable," said Bertie.

"You smell like one," replied Nick. "Anyway, I bet I could beat you."

"No chance," said Bertie.

"Want to bet?" said Nick. "First one to cross the finish line wins."

"You're on," said Bertie, shaking hands.

"And the loser…" Nick thought for a minute. "The loser has to kiss Miss Boot!"

Bertie almost choked. Kiss Miss Boot? He'd rather kiss Angela Nicely! Come to that, he'd rather kiss Darren!

"What's the matter — backing out, scaredy cat?" jeered Nick.

"Course not," said Bertie.

"Good, then I'll see you Friday. Better get in some practice, kissy lips!"

Bertie glared after him.

"Yikes!" said Eugene. "You wouldn't really?"

"What?" said Bertie.

"Kiss Miss Boot?"

"No way," said Bertie. "But I won't have to cos I'm going to win."

"But say you lost," said Darren. "You'd actually have to kiss her. I mean, Miss Boot!"

"Okay, stop going on about it!" said

Bertie. He was starting to feel sick. "Anyway, it's only Know-All Nick. He may be the class brainiac but he runs like a penguin. There's no way he'll beat me at cross-country."

Bertie folded his arms. He was almost looking forward to Friday. This time Nick had picked the wrong bet. He'd never been sporty. If you threw him a ball he practically screamed. Five minutes of cross-country and he'd be begging to stop.

Bertie couldn't wait to see Nick try to kiss Miss Boot. She'd probably flatten him with her handbag.

CHAPTER 3

On Friday morning Bertie wolfed down his breakfast. As usual he was late for school.

"Oh, I need my PE kit today," he said.

Mum rolled her eyes. "Why didn't you say so last night?"

"I forgot," said Bertie. "We're doing cross-country with Miss Boot."

Dirty Bertie

Suzy looked up. "You can't be serious!" she said.

"Why not?" said Bertie.

"Do you actually know what cross-country is?" asked Suzy.

"Course I do, it's a sort of race," said Bertie.

"Yes, a race that lasts for HOURS," said Suzy.

"I'm sure it can't be that bad," said Mum. "These socks are filthy, Bertie!"

"I'm telling you, cross-country is murder," said Suzy. "It should be against the law."

"How do you know so much?" asked Bertie.

"Because we did it last year. I almost died," said Suzy. "Bella was off sick for a week!"

Bertie glanced out of the window at the grey sky. Maybe Miss Boot would put off cross-country till another day? Anyway, it was too late to back out now – he had to beat Know-All Nick and win the bet.

Bertie stood on the starting line with the rest of Class 3. A biting wind swept across Deadwood Country Park. The sky had turned black and the first drops of rain were falling. Bertie shivered in his T-shirt and shorts.

"Can't we run somewhere else?" he asked. "Like indoors?"

"Don't be silly," snapped Miss Boot. "It's cross-country, not tiddlywinks."

"But it's raining, Miss," moaned Eugene.

"And muddy!" grumbled Darren.

"A bit of mud never hurt anyone," said Miss Boot. "When I was at school we used to run when we were up to our knees in snow – and we enjoyed it. Now listen, follow the yellow arrows and you can't get lost."

Bertie looked down the hill. "How far is it?" he asked.

"Not far – three kilometres," said Miss Boot.

THREE KILOMETRES? Had Miss Boot lost her mind? On Sports Day they

Dirty Bertie

raced sixty metres and Bertie was out
of breath. They'd never make it back…
They'd die! Where was the ambulance
crew standing by with stretchers?

Know-All Nick pushed in beside
Bertie. His PE kit shone whiter than his
legs and he was wearing mittens.

"Ready for this, Bertie?" he smirked. "I hope you haven't forgotten our little bet. Last one back has to kiss Miss Boot."

"Good luck with that," said Bertie.

He pulled up his shorts, which were flapping in the wind. Nick wouldn't last long. He hated getting cold and dirty, so beating him shouldn't be difficult. Bertie would set off fast and open up a big lead. Then he could take his time and still cross the line first.

Miss Boot raised her arm. "On your marks, get set ... GO!"

Class 3 set off down the hill, bunched together like sardines.

"RUN!" roared Miss Boot. "GET A MOVE ON!"

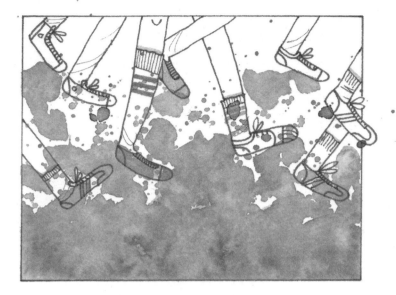

CHAPTER 4

Bertie looked round for Nick. He was tucked in just behind him. They splashed downhill.

At the bottom, the track curved left beside a muddy duck pond. Nick put on a burst of speed to draw level with Bertie. There was barely room for two of them on the path.

Dirty Bertie

Nick pointed. "Look, a crocodile!" he cried.

"Where?" said Bertie, turning his head.

SPLASH!

Nick gave him a violent shove so that he toppled into the pond. The ducks swam round him, quacking in protest.

Dirty Bertie

Bertie clambered out of the pond, dripping wet. He would get Nick for this.

SPLODGE, SPLODGE, SPLODGE!

It took Bertie a while to catch up. His trainers were full of water. He could see his enemy ahead, climbing a steep hill. Nick paused and hung on to a low branch, panting heavily.

"Get a move on, slow coach!" he called.

Bertie hurried up the hill. Nick waited until he drew close, then let go of the branch he was holding.

THWACK! It sprang back, whacking Bertie in the face.

"ARGH!" He slipped and rolled back down the hill.

"HA! HA! No time to lie down, Bertie!" jeered Nick.

Bertie picked himself up. He was now
soaked through and muddy as a pig.
He would catch up with that two-faced
sneak if it killed him. He staggered back
up the hill.

Bertie splodged on through the mud.
How much further? It felt like he'd been
running for days.

Call this sport? thought Bertie. *More*

like torture. He bet none of his teachers did cross-country. The nearest Miss Boot got to exercise was reaching for another biscuit.

He'd lost sight of the other runners. They were probably somewhere up ahead. But where was Know-All Nick? He couldn't be that far ahead could he? What if he was out of the woods – or even close to the finish! Bertie staggered on. If he lost he'd have to KISS Miss Boot – in front of everyone! No, it was too ghastly to imagine.

Wait, there was Nick! He was dragging himself along, looking fit to collapse.

Bertie caught up with him. "Getting tired, Nickerless?" he grinned.

"Never!" panted Nick. "I'm … just …

getting … started."

The track led through the woods beside a field. There was a large sign on the fence:

PRIVATE PROPERTY – NO ENTRY – KEEP OUT!

Bertie glanced round. He could take a shortcut across the field. The finish line was at the top of the hill. In a few minutes he could be there. Wouldn't Nick turn green when he realized he'd lost? Bertie climbed the fence.

"Wait! Where are you going?" wailed Nick. "That's not the right way!"

"It's the way I'm going," said Bertie. "First to the finish – that was the bet. No one said anything about keeping to the course."

Nick looked round. He didn't want

to get into trouble but he couldn't let Bertie win. Besides, a shortcut meant the race would be over quicker.

"Hey! Wait for me!" he yelled.

Dirty Bertie

Bertie jogged across the field, skipping over cowpats. This was easy. Once he saw the finish line he'd sprint, leaving Nick way behind. No contest.

"What is this field anyway?" asked Nick.

Bertie shrugged. "Just a cow field. But luckily there aren' t any … oh." He gulped. A large herd of cows stood blocking their way. Up close, cows were much bigger than you'd think – and these ones didn't look pleased to see them.

Dirty Bertie

Nick grabbed Bertie's arm. "Let's go back."

"They're only cows," said Bertie. "They're probably scared of us."

"They don't look scared," said Nick. "That one's got horns."

"Which one?" said Bertie.

"That black one there."

Bertie's eyes grew wide. "That isn't a cow," he said. "RUN FOR IT!"

Dirty Bertie

They tore across the field. Bertie
looked behind him. The bull – it was
definitely a bull – was charging after
them with its head down. The ground
shook as it thundered closer.

"Help! Mummy!" wailed Nick.

"Make for the fence!" panted Bertie.
Bertie got there first and dived over,
landing in a puddle.

A moment later Nick
crashed on top
of him.

Dirty Bertie

"ARGH! OWW!"

They didn't stop to look back. They kept running until they passed between two white posts. Bertie crossed the finish line just in front.

Miss Boot stepped out to greet them, beaming happily.

"Well done, Bertie! Third place," she said. "And you were a close fourth, Nicholas."

"Third?" wheezed Bertie.

"Yes, which means you'll both be running for the school cross-country team," said Miss Boot.

Bertie groaned. More cross-country? More cold and rain and slogging through miles of mud? Could anything be worse? Well, actually, come to think of it, there was one thing.

"Oh Nickerless, remember our little bet?" said Bertie. "I won. Isn't there something you'd like to give Miss Boot?"

"Oh? What's that?" demanded Miss Boot.

Nick had gone red. He backed away in horror, then turned and fled. Bertie grinned. Actually, Nick could run pretty fast when he wanted to.

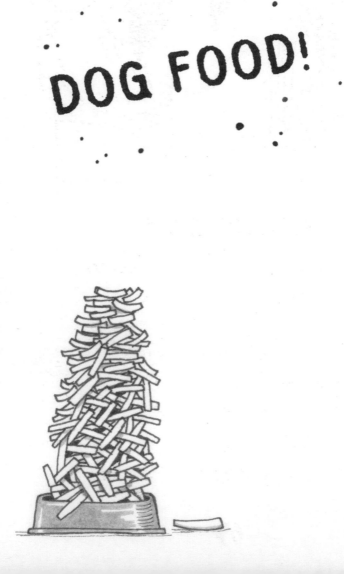

CHAPTER 1

Bertie waited anxiously for the vet to finish his examination. Mr Cage and Whiffer were old enemies. But today Whiffer hadn't whined or even tried to bolt out of the door.

"You say he doesn't like going for walks?" asked Mr Cage.

"Not really," said Bertie. "Half the

time he just stops and sits down. I think he expects me to carry him."

"I see," said the vet. "And he's not off his food?"

"Not a bit," answered Dad.

"He eats everything – chips are his favourite," said Bertie.

Mr Cage stood up. "Well there's your problem," he said. "He's too fat."

"FAT?" said Bertie.

"You probably haven't noticed," said Mr Cage. "People often don't when their dogs put on weight."

Dad sighed. "So he's not actually sick or anything?" he said.

"Oh no," replied Mr Cage. "He just eats too much."

Bertie looked relieved.

Fat – was that all?

Bertie had been worried that Whiffer was ill, with something like measles, chicken pox or maybe doggy pox. But it turned out he'd just put on weight. Come to think of it, Whiffer did spend hours dozing in front of the TV.

But so what? Loads of pets were a bit porky. Angela Nicely's cat could hardly squeeze through the cat flap.

"So what should we do about it?"

Dad asked.

"Put him on a strict diet," said the vet. "Two light meals a day and plenty of healthy walks. Cut out the snacking too."

"Hear that Bertie? No more chips," said Dad.

Bertie nodded. It wasn't always chips anyway – sometimes it was pepperoni pizza.

They set off home. Whiffer trailed behind, panting as if he'd just run a marathon. Eventually he sat down and refused to budge.

"Come on!" moaned Bertie, pulling at the lead.

"See?" said Dad. "He's a big lazy lump."

"Don't say that! He'll hear you!" said
Bertie.

"Well it's true – and it's our fault,"
sighed Dad. "Yours especially."

"ME? What did I do?" cried Bertie.

"He's your dog. You should take care
of him," said Dad.

"I do!" argued Bertie. "I'm the one
that feeds him!"

"Yes, and he eats too much," said Dad.

"From tomorrow he starts his diet."

Bertie rolled his eyes. It was all very well saying it, but getting Whiffer to cut down was another matter. He loved eating and he didn't love exercise.

"Come on boy, let's go home," said Bertie.

Whiffer raised a paw and scratched his ear.

"That won't work, you have to order him," said Dad.

"COME ON, WHIFFER! GET A MOVE ON!" Bertie pulled hard on the dog lead. Whiffer got up, walked as far as the next lamp post, then sat down again.

"Hmm," said Bertie. "It might be quicker to carry him."

CHAPTER 2

"Supper's READY!"

Bertie skidded into the kitchen and landed on a chair. "Yum! Sausages and mash!" he said.

"Sit up straight and take your elbows off the table," ordered Mum.

Bertie sighed. He couldn't even sit down without getting in trouble. One

day he was going to open a restaurant
where table manners would be banned.

"So how is Whiffer's diet going?"
asked Dad.

"Fine," said Bertie. "Except he's always
hungry."

"You've got to be firm with him," said
Mum.

"I *am* firm," insisted Bertie.

Something warm was pressing against
his leg. He looked down to discover
Whiffer hiding under the table.

"Where is he anyway?" asked Mum.

"Who?" asked Bertie.

"Whiffer."

Bertie glanced down. "In the garden
probably." Since the diet began Whiffer
wasn't allowed in the kitchen at
mealtimes.

"Anyway I think he's lost weight," Bertie said.

Suzy laughed. "I doubt it," she said.

"But he looks thinner – especially when he's lying down," argued Bertie.

Whiffer was gazing up at him with big sad eyes. He could smell freshly cooked sausages – his second favourite food after chips.

"He's got to learn to cut down," said Dad.

"He is," said Bertie. "I hardly put anything in his bowl."

Dirty Bertie

No one was looking. He speared a sausage on his fork and lowered it under the table. Whiffer saw it and licked his lips…

"What are you doing?"

Uh oh – Suzy was staring at him.

"Nothing!" said Bertie.

"You are, you've got something under the table," said Suzy.

Mum leaned down, just in time to see Whiffer wolfing down the last of the sausage.

"BERTIE!" she groaned. "What did we say about feeding him at the table?"

"I couldn't help it," said Bertie. "He was begging me!"

Dad took Whiffer by the collar and led him out. He closed the door behind the dog.

Mum shook her head. "You're not
helping him, Bertie," she said. "Do you
want him to be overweight?"

"No! But he's hungry," said Bertie.

"Greedy more like," said Dad. "He
has to stick to his diet."

Bertie sighed heavily. Whiffer had
only been on his diet for two days but
already it seemed like a year. Whenever
Bertie got back from school Whiffer was

waiting by his dog bowl. He followed
Bertie all round the house – even to the
toilet. It was driving him up the wall.

"By the way, the Nicelys are coming
to supper tomorrow," said Mum.

Suzy groaned. Bertie almost choked
on his food.

"What for?" he moaned.

"I invited them," said Mum. "I thought
we should get to know them better."

Bertie thought he'd rather get to
know the Nicelys less. It was bad
enough that they lived next door!
Besides, they'd probably bring Angela,
who'd want him to play mummies and
daddies. He'd just have to keep out of
the way till they'd gone.

"Can I eat in my room?" he asked.

"Of course not! You'll eat with us,"

Dirty Bertie

said Mum.

"It won't kill you," said Dad.

"You'd better mind your manners too," warned Mum. "And keep Whiffer out of the way – you know how Mrs Nicely feels about dogs."

Bertie slumped back in his seat. A meal with adoring Angela and her boring parents – could anything be worse?

CHAPTER 3

Bertie looked at the clock. The Nicelys
would be here in half an hour. There
had to be some way to get out of
it. Maybe he could pretend to have
toothache? No, last time he tried that
Mum booked him an appointment with
the dentist. Wait a minute – hadn't
she told him to keep Whiffer out of

the way? That was it! He rushed down to the kitchen, where Mum was busy making supper.

"I just remembered," he said. "Whiffer hasn't had a walk."

"It's too late now," said Mum.

"Can't I just take him round the block?" begged Bertie. "The vet said he needs to go everyday."

"You should have done it earlier," said Mum. "Now go and get changed, and take Whiffer with you. I don't want him in here while there's food around."

Bertie dragged himself upstairs. There was no escape. At least Mum was cooking one of his favourite meals – shepherd's pie. He had seen it on the side, ready to go in the oven.

Once he had changed, Bertie settled

on the lounge sofa to watch TV. Whiffer hung around, looking pathetic. He'd finished the food in his bowl and wanted more. Bertie ignored him – he'd give up eventually. But ten minutes into the programme, he looked around. Uh oh – where was that dopey dog?

Bertie dashed into the kitchen. Whiffer had his paws on the worktop and was guzzling something with loud slurps.

"NO! GET DOWN!" cried Bertie, pulling him off. He looked at the dish.

AARGHHH! MUM'S SHEPHERD'S PIE! The one they were having for supper!

Whiffer looked pleased with himself. He had gravy round his mouth and a blob of mashed potato on his nose.

Dirty Bertie

"Bad boy!" said Bertie, wagging a finger. "GO ON! OUT!"

Whiffer ran off. Bertie examined the shepherd's pie. It was a disaster. There was a gaping hole in the middle where Whiffer had been nosing. The smooth mash topping looked like a bomb crater. Bertie put a hand to his head. What on earth was he going to do? Any minute now the Nicelys would arrive and there'd be nothing to give them.

Unless... Bertie thought quickly — maybe the damage could be repaired? First he'd have to fill in the hole. But what with? He looked in the food cupboard. Jam? Porridge? No, of course, peanut butter — brown and easy to spread! He took a spoonful and blobbed it in. Might as well use the whole jar.

Once it was
done, he
smoothed
over the
mashed potato
to cover his work. The pie still looked
like a gloopy mess but it was better than
nothing.

Someone was coming. He shoved the
pie in the oven and slammed the door,
just in time.

Mum looked around. "Where's my
shepherd's pie?" she asked.

"Oh, I put it in the oven for you,"
replied Bertie.

Mum frowned. "I told you not to
touch anything," she said, turning the
oven up. "And where's that dog? I don't
want him here when the Nicelys arrive."

CHAPTER 4

Bertie sat at the table, sandwiched between Suzy and Angela. He ate a spoonful of tomato soup.

Suzy shot him a look. "Don't slurp!" she hissed.

Bertie stuck out his tongue. Angela hadn't stopped talking since she'd arrived but he hadn't listened to a word. He was

too worried about the shepherd's pie
in the oven. Maybe it wouldn't look so
bad once it was cooked? Or maybe the
Nicelys would be so busy talking they
wouldn't notice anything? If Mum knew
what Whiffer had done she would go
bananas! And Bertie was bound to get
the blame. He felt sick. Perhaps he could
ask to be excused?

Angela was staring at him. "You're
very quiet today," she said.

"Am I?" mumbled Bertie.

"Don't you like tomato soup? I've
eaten all mine!" said Angela.

Dad collected up their bowls.

Here it comes, thought Bertie.

Mum went over to the oven and
brought out the shepherd's pie.

"Oh! Good heavens!" she gasped.

Dirty Bertie

The pie looked even worse than Bertie remembered. It seemed to have suffered some sort of landslide. Gravy dripped down one side of the dish. The Nicelys stared at it boggle-eyed.

Dirty Bertie

"Goodness ... how unusual," said Mrs Nicely.

"What is it?" asked Angela.

"Shepherd's pie," said Mum, weakly. "It was fine when it went in the oven. I can't think what could have happened."

Bertie avoided her eye.

Mr Nicely laughed. "Well I'm sure it tastes delicious," he said.

I wouldn't bet on it, thought Bertie.

Mum served up the pie and passed round their plates.

Bertie held his breath. This was it — they were actually going to eat it!

The Nicelys raised their forks and chewed their food in silence. Bertie waited. No one choked or spat it out. Mrs Nicely pulled a face.

"What an … um … interesting flavour!" she said.

"Yes, it tastes sort of nutty," said Mr Nicely.

Angela nudged Bertie. "Aren't you eating any?" she asked.

"Course I am," said Bertie. "I'm just … letting it cool down."

He breathed a sigh of relief. It was going to be okay. The shepherd's pie wouldn't win any prizes but no one suspected the truth…

Dirty Bertie

"URGH!" Mrs Nicely let out a sudden squawk.

Her husband looked up. "Oh dear, darling, are you all right?"

Mrs Nicely shook her head and pulled something out of her mouth. Bertie stared at it in horror. It was a long, white hair — exactly like the dog-hairs on the sofa.

"EWWW!" cried Suzy.

"YUCK!" cried Angela.

Mrs Nicely had gone a funny shade of green.

Mum rose to her feet. "I am SO sorry!" she said. "I don't know how it got in there. It's certainly not one of mine!"

At that moment Whiffer trotted in.

He still had gravy stains round his mouth.
Mum stared. A horrible thought crept
into her mind.

The same horrible thought struck
Mrs Nicely. She dropped her fork and
clutched at her throat. "THE DOG!" she
gasped. "I think I'm going to be SICK!"

Dirty Bertie

The Nicelys did not stay for dessert.
Mrs Nicely said she would never be able
to look at a shepherd's pie again. She
needed to go home and lie down.

Mum tried to apologize while Dad
went to fetch the Nicelys' coats.

At the front door Angela turned
round. "Thank you for having me," she
said politely. "But next time…"

"ANGELA!" snapped her mother.
"We are going home!"

The front door slammed. Mum and
Dad looked at each other.

"BERTIE!" yelled Mum.

They marched into the kitchen. But
the back door was open and Bertie
wasn't there. He'd just remembered

Dirty Bertie

something — Whiffer needed a walk and there was no time like the present.